LIZ GARTON SCANLON

I Want a Boat!

Pictures by
KEVAN ATTEBERRY

NEAL PORTER BOOKS
HOLIDAY HOUSE / NEW YORK

For my VCFA community—here's to thinking outside the box —L.G.S.

For Ella —K.A.

Neal Porter Books

Text copyright © 2121 by Liz Garton Scanlon
Illustrations copyright © 2121 by Kevan Atteberry
All Rights Reserved
HOLIDAY HOUSE is registered in the U.S. Patent and Trademark Office.
Printed and bound in February 2021 at C & C Offset, Shenzhen, China.
The artwork for this book was created with watercolor and acrylics, as well as digital tools.
www.holidayhouse.com
First Edition
1   3   5   7   9   10   8   6   4   2
Library of Congress Cataloging-in-Publication Data

Names: Scanlon, Elizabeth Garton, author. | Atteberry, Kevan, illustrator.
Title: I want a boat / by Liz Garton Scanlon ; illustrated by Kevan Atteberry.
Description: First edition. | New York : Holiday House, [2021] | "A Neal
Porter Book." | Audience: Ages 4 to 8. | Audience: Grades K–1. |
Summary: A girl uses her imagination to turn an ordinary box into a sailboat.
Identifiers: LCCN 2020025840 | ISBN 9780823447152 (hardcover)
Subjects: CYAC: Imagination—Fiction. | Sailboats—Fiction.
Classification: LCC PZ7.S2798 Iaw 2021 | DDC [E]—dc23
LC record available at https://lccn.loc.gov/2020025840

ISBN 978-0-8234-4715-2 (hardcover)

I have a box.
I want a boat.

I have a boat.
I want a rudder.

I have a rudder.
I want a sail.

I have a sail.

I want the sea!

I have the sea.
I want a map.

I have a map.
I want a crew.

I have a crew.

I have the wind.

I want the world.

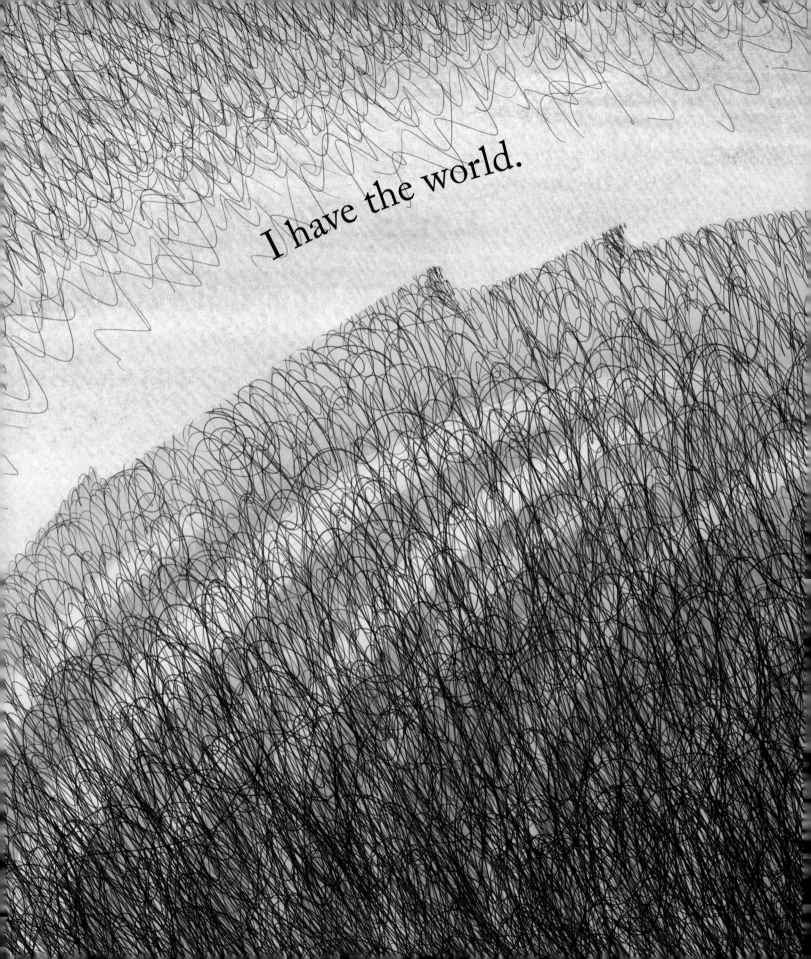

I have the world.

I want the sky.

I have the sky.

I want a storm.

I have a storm.

I have some light.
I want my crew.

I have my crew.
I want the map.

I have the map.

I want the shore.

I have the shore.

I want my supper.

I have my supper.
I want to sleep.

I've gone to sleep.
I want to dream.

I have a . . .

box.